AF653955

CHAMPAK

FUN TRAIN YOUR BRAIN

MOONSTONE

Published by
Rupa Publications India Pvt. Ltd 2023
161-B/4, Gulmohar House,
Yusuf Sarai Community Centre,
New Delhi 110049

Sales centres:
Bengaluru Chennai
Hyderabad Kolkata Mumbai

P-ISBN: 978-93-5702-434-1
E-ISBN: 978-93-5702-380-1

Fifth impression 2026

10 9 8 7 6 5

Printed in India

Colour this picture with cool-toned colours only

Complete the Picture

June 1 is World Milk Day. Parts of this image has been left blank. Look at the picture, complete it, and then colour it.

Decode Me

Astronaut Heidi has spilt her chocolate milkshake in space. Use the code to solve the riddle and find out what happens when an astronaut lets go of her milkshake.

Colour this picture with bright colours

Maze

World Habitat Day is celebrated on October 7. Help the animals find shelter in their respective habitats.

Complete the Picture

Parts of this image have been left blank. Look at the picture, complete it, and then colour it.

Complete the Word

Each of these words has a name of an animal in it. Can you sound out the words and complete them?

 + d = ______________

 + htub = ______________

Va +  + ion = ______________

 + ded = ______________

Butter +  = ______________

Star +  = ______________

Hot +  = ______________

 + shoe = ______________

Colour using primary colours

Odd One Out

Rehan is learning about different groups of animals. Help him by circling the wrong animal in each group.

Amphibians

Mammals

Reptiles

Insects

Birds

Follow Me

Which way should the leader of these elephants go to take their herd to the river?

Colour using sketch pens

Dot to Dot

Join the dots to find out what the ants are carrying.

Rebus

This story has been written using both pictures and words. Enjoy reading it!

One day ,a  saw 2  . They were fighting

over a  . " 

fighting ," the  said. " 

will divide this  for U." The 

believed the  and let him pick up the

 . But to their surprise, the 

took the  and ran away. " Oh no,"

the  cried. " Had we not

fought, or believed the  , we

would still have had our lunch!"

Colour using crayons

Maze

Help this snail catch up with her friends who are waiting for her.

Maze

Let the playful nature of rats enchant you and help you discover the joy of keeping them as pets. Discover the mouth-watering treats Sophia has prepared for her adorable pet Rony. Join the fun now!

Fill in the Blanks

Fill in the blanks by choosing an answer from the word bank below.

1. A ________ of bees

2. A ________ of crows

3. A ________ of cats

4. A ________ of chicks

5. A ________ of whales

6. A ________ of hawks

7. A ________ of lions

8. A ________ of owls

FLIGHT LITTER SCHOOL PARLIAMENT

CLUTCH MURDER PRIDE KETTLE

Colour this picture with warm colours

Complete the Picture

Parts of this image have been left blank. Look at the picture, complete it, and then colour it.

Maze

Help the mother spider reach her baby through the spider web.

Colour this picture with warm colours

Maze

Help this Siamese cat find its way to its twin.

- Siamese cats originated from Thailand and have a rich history dating to the 1300's.
- Known as one of the most vocal cats, their sound ranges from soft meows to loud wails.
- Siamese are affectionate and intelligent cats.

Solve It

The last male northern white rhino passed away on March 19, 2018, taking this species closer to extinction. In the rows given below, circle the species that is extinct.

African Elephant

Polar Bear

Pyrenean Ibex

Snow Leopard

House Sparrow

Dodo

Penguin

Great Indian Bustard

Peacock

Indian Vulture

Indian Eagle Owl

Passenger Pigeon

Hippopotamus

Quagga

Wild Water Buffalo

Zebra

Checkers

Help the little chick find its way to the coop. The one who finishes first wins the game!

You will need:

1. Pegs for each player
2. Dice

Instructions:

1. Start playing when your dice rolls 3.
2. Then roll it again and move your peg according to the number of spaces it shows.
3. If you run into a hungry fox, you will have to move back two spaces.
4. If you run into a greedy cat, you will miss a turn.
5. If you land on a juicy worm or bird seed, you can move an extra space forward.

Complete the Picture

Parts of this image have been left blank. Look at the picture, complete it, and then colour it.

Decode Me

This beautiful flower is named after something children love to eat. write the first letter of the objects shown below to find out its name.

One of Cheeku's favourite places is the garden. He's written a note telling you why. But some letters are missing. Find them and fill in the blank. Once it is complete, read the note.

One of the places I like visiting is the ☐arden. It is full of ☐resh and clean ☐ir. The flo☐ers that bloom in the garden make it a pretty sight.

I see many beautifu☐ birds sitting on the trees. Their c☐eerful singing makes me feel happy.

I have many little friends like the s☐uirrel, the earth☐orms, the snai☐s, the g☐sshopper, the bee☐les and the ☐utterflies. I get to meet them when I'm here.

Since the garden is bi☐ and open, there's plenty of place for me to ☐xercise and pla☐. Why don't you join me in the garden some time? It will be ☐un.

Dot to Dot

Join the dots to find out what everyone is laughing at.

Dot to Dot

Join the dots.

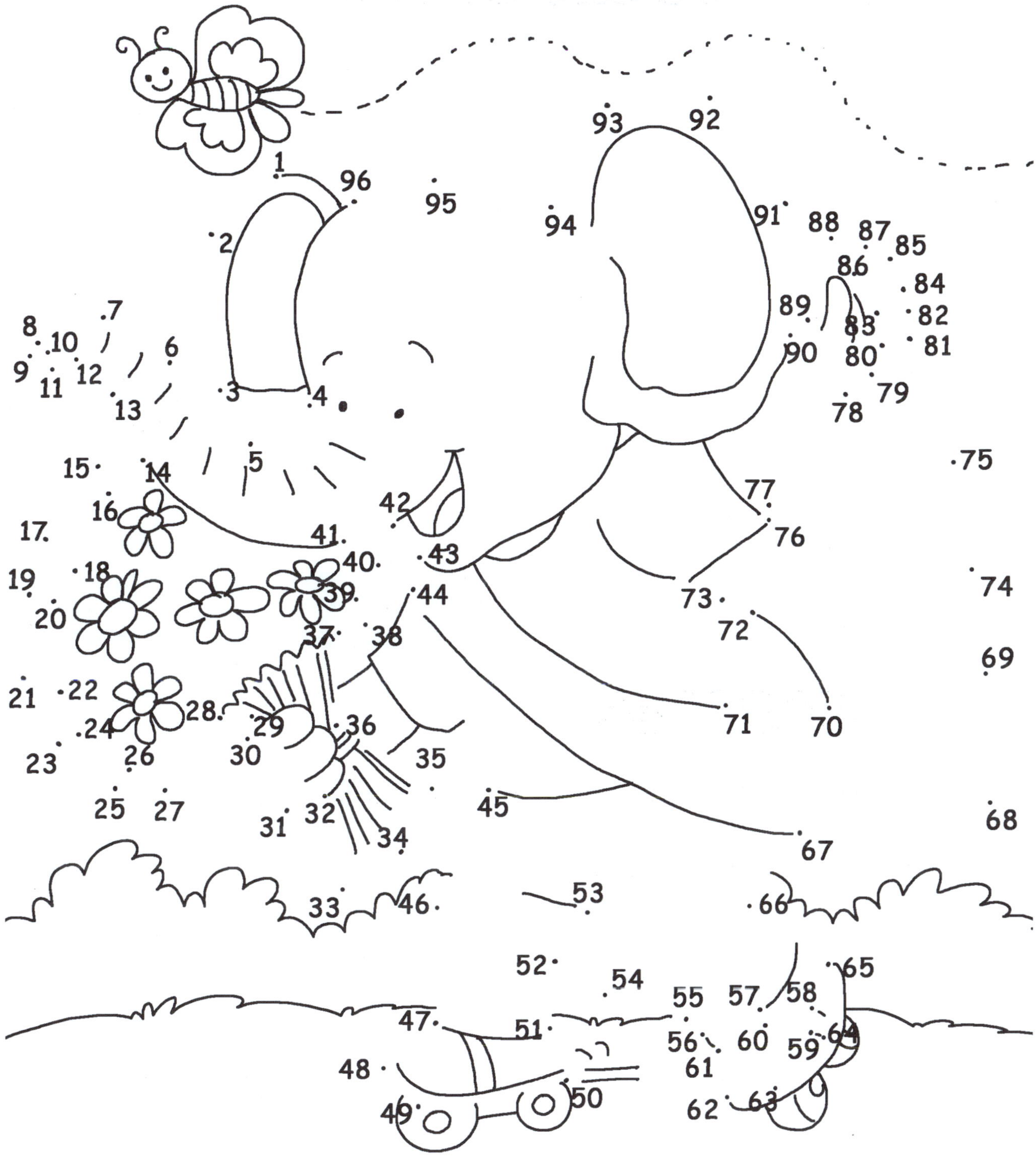

Solve It

Flower Search

T P C S V I O L E T
U D A F F O D I L P
L P R H D A H L I A
I Y N E N S Z Y O R
P F A O B L Q Y A S
U L T O C D A I S Y
R E I J X K M T T F
O R O R C H I D E O
S U N F L O W E R W
E D A N D E L I O N

The children are surrounded by beautiful flowers. Can you find their names?

BUSY BEE

Help this hungry bee find which flower is the sweetest of all!

Hint

- The difference between the two digits of this number is 3.
- It is an odd number.
- The total of the two digits is 5.

Maze

These birds are off on a holiday to a warmer place. Which route should they take? Show them the way by filling in the arrows in the blank circles. We have helped you get started.

Decode Me

Secret Code

Six songbirds have been shown here. Their names are written in pictures. Break the code to find out what the names are?

A 

Answer: CUCKOO

B 

Answer:

C 

Answer:

D 

Answer:

E 

Answer:

F 

Answer:

Hint: 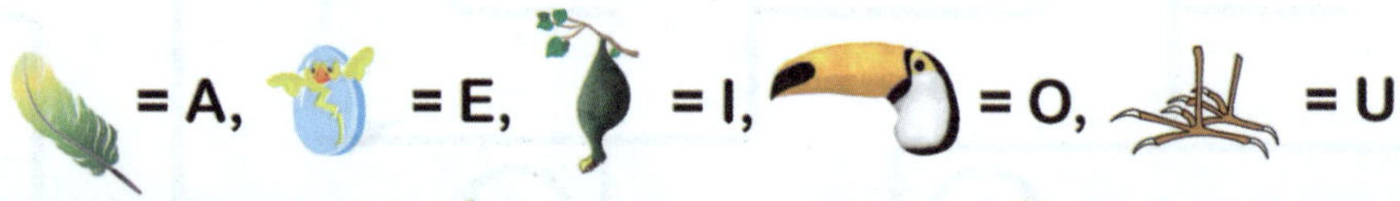

K	M	N	O	P
P	O	I	N	M
N	M	Z	P	O
Z	W	Y	B	I

Cross Out

The name of this flightless bird found in New Zealand is hidden in the gird below. Follow the instructions to find it.

Instructions:

- First cross out all the Bs, Zs and Ys in the grid.
- Then cross out all the Ms and Ns.
- Now cross out the vowels Os and Ps
- Unscramble the remaining alphabets to from the name of of the bird.

Solve It

Complete the pattern of the fruit sticks by drawing the missing fruits till the end of the skewers

Fun with Fruits

Solve It

Science Homework

Meeku mouse is completing his science homework and needs some help. Complete the following equations on water.

Fix the Recipe

Blacky bear is making some hot *puris* for his friends for Diwali, but his recipe book has some ingredients missing, can you look at the pictures and complete the ingredients list to help Blacky?

Word Search

April 18 is World Heritage Day. In the grid below, find the names of some World Heritage Sites in India.

1) _LE_H_N_ _ Caves

2) K_AJ_R_ _O Temples

3) _A_P_ Group of Monuments

4) F_T_H_UR SIKRI

5) T_J M_HA_

6) _OD_ G_Y_

7) R_N_ KI V_V

B	E	S	W	B	U	A	S	D	E	B
O	L	H	E	A	T	P	R	P	L	K
D	E	O	S	R	T	A	B	C	E	H
H	P	F	A	T	E	H	P	U	R	A
G	H	I	L	A	K	C	A	O	B	J
A	A	L	K	H	A	M	P	I	A	U
Y	N	N	D	E	Y	K	I	I	N	R
A	T	T	A	J	M	A	H	A	L	A
N	A	V	A	X	H	A	A	N	A	H
M	B	R	P	U	S	U	Q	Y	L	O
Z	R	A	N	I	K	I	V	A	V	L

Dot to Dot

Join the dots to find out what everyone is laughing at.

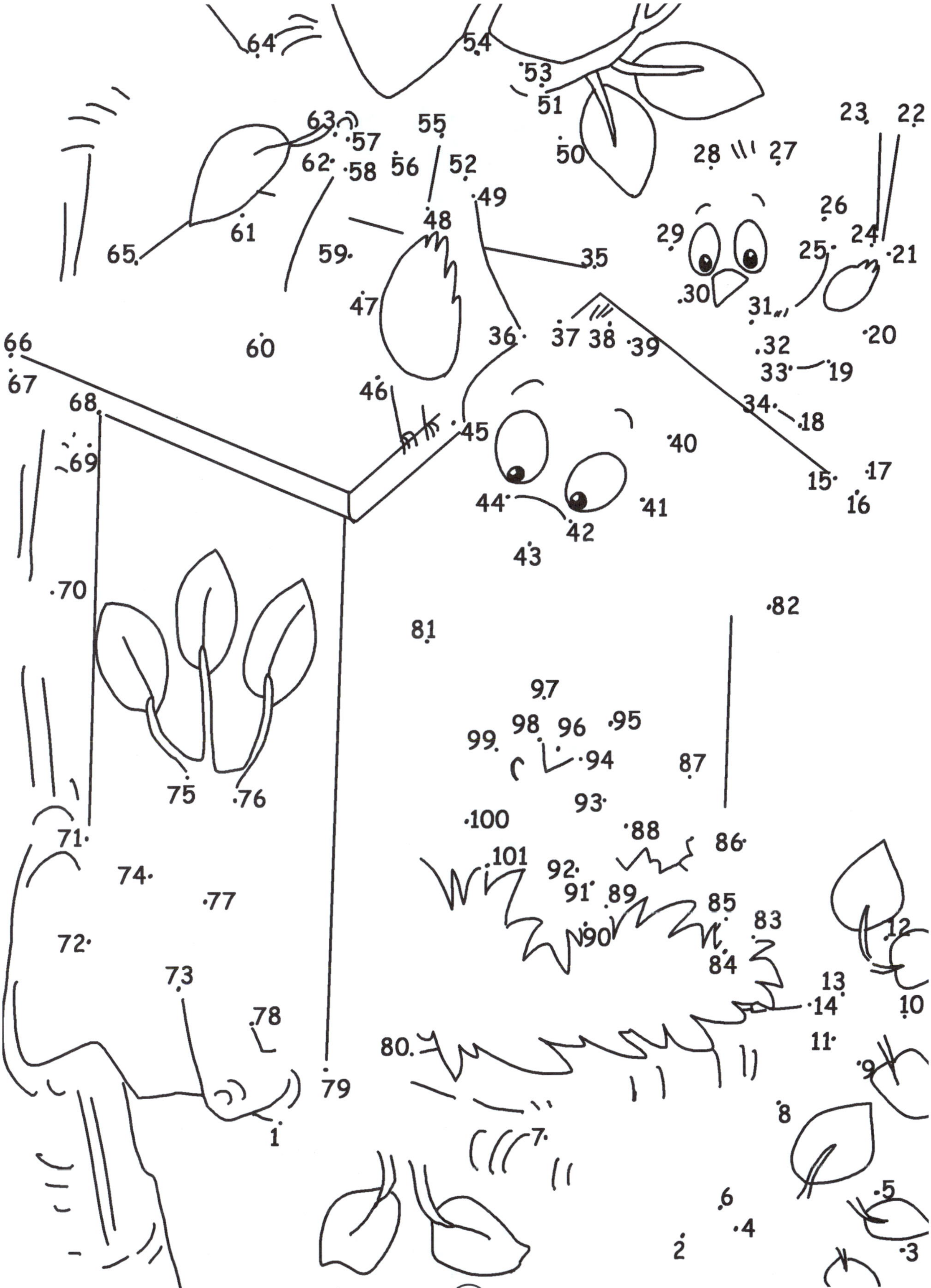

Unscramble

Rearrange the words and match them to the correct picture.

1. ceapock
2. lebmem
3. ulsot
4. anghdi
5. anbyan etre
6. ngmoa
7. eocyhk
8. getir

A

B

D

C

F

E

G

H

Maze

Help Maya, who likes to keep fit, find her way to the yoga class.

Dot to Dot

Join the dots to find out why everyone is laughing

Complete the Picture

Parts of this image have been left blank. Look at the picture, complete it, and then colour it.

Maze

As part of the World Athletics Championship, three athletes are participating in the race. Identify which one of them will take the fastest route to win the race.

Memory

June 21 is International Yoga Day. Observe the picture for a minute, cover it, and try answering the questions given in the box.

Q1. How many people are practicing yoga in the first row?

Q2. What is written on the board near the instructor?

Q3. How many boats can you count?

Complete the Picture

Parts of this image have been left blank. Look at the picture, complete it, and then colour it.

Activity Therapy

The names of some activities that can keep your mind and body healthy are hidden in the grid below. Can you find them?

Look at the illustrations for hints.

C	H	P	A	M	P	Y	S	M
Y	O	G	A	U	R	A	W	N
C	D	I	R	S	E	B	I	O
L	E	J	Q	I	A	A	M	P
I	E	K	P	C	D	Z	M	Q
N	T	E	N	N	I	S	I	R
G	F	L	O	S	N	Y	N	S
H	T	M	N	T	G	X	G	T
K	A	R	A	T	E	W	V	U

Run Along

Cheeku and Blacky are having a race. Figure out the length of the track (in miles) by multiplying the two numbers that appear four times on the race track. Once you find these numbers, multiply them to know the answer.

2	7	6	5	4	3
1	9	8	2	0	7
1	2	2	4	9	3
4	0	8	7	4	5

Dot to Dot

Join the dots.

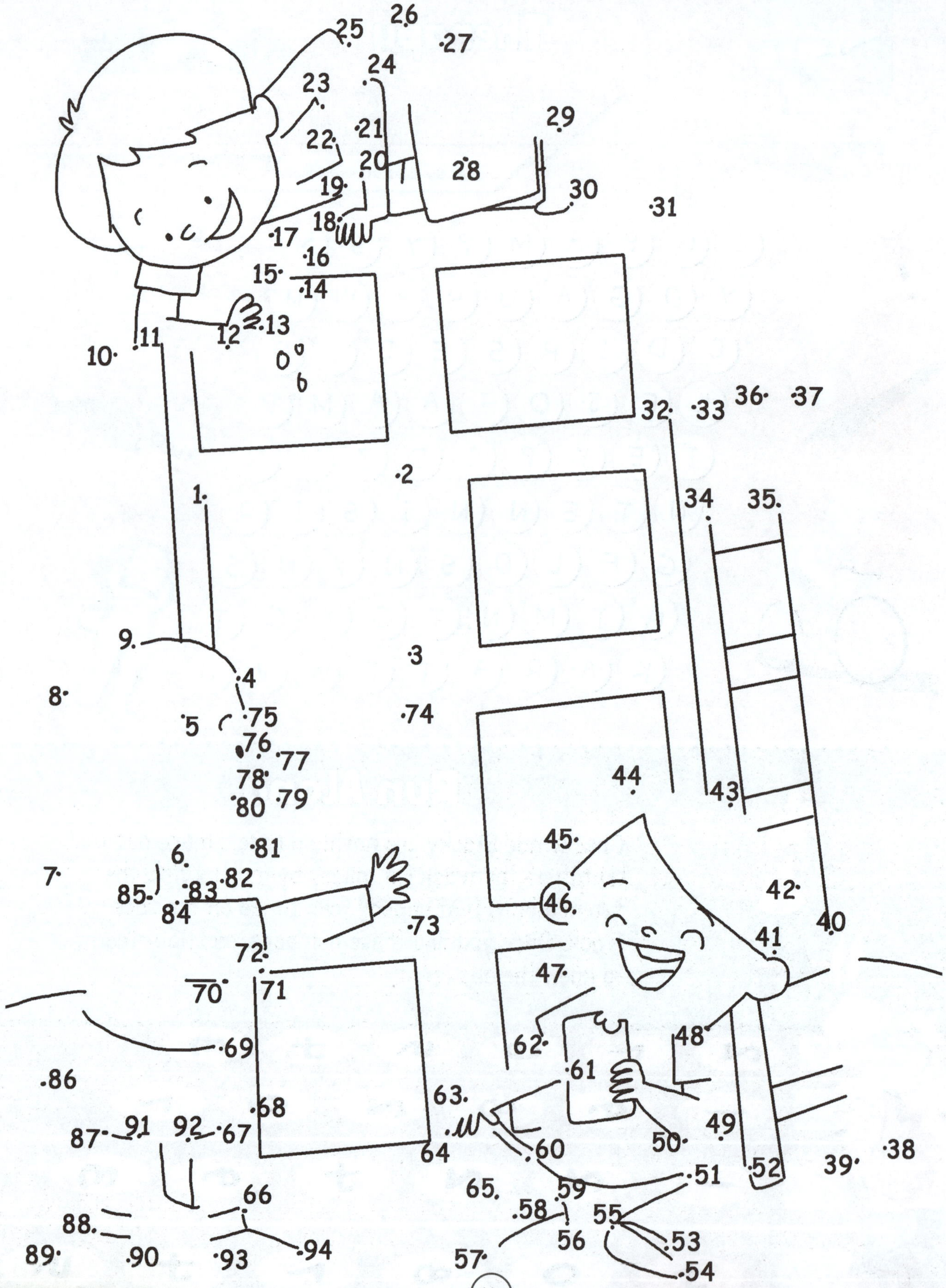

Solve It

Bird Beep

As winter approaches, many birds migrate from one country to another. Tiya Crane is migrating with her flock. Her friends have sent her a message that Tiya is unable to read. Using the answer key, help Tiya decode the message.

Code: 96 9844 5877 231

Colour using poster paints

National Sports Day is on August 29.

Maze

Help this tired race car find its way to the pit stop so that it can recharge for the race.

Time to Refresh

Dot to Dot

Join the dots to find out what Cheeku and Jumbo are doing.

Solve It

Change Challenge

Line up these six coins as per the clues given below

1 - Together, the first and last coins total rupees 12.

2 - The last coin is worth more than the first.

3 - The second coin is worth more than the third.

4 - The fourth coin is worth half as much as the fifth coin.

In or Out?

Add each letter to the "In" or "Out" to form new words.
Some words are "In" and some words are "Out".
Some words go in both "In" and "Out"

Example: TH goes in "In"
Th + In = Thin

Unscramble

Some very healthy foods have been shown here. But their names have scrambled. Can you unscramble them and write the names in the blank spaces?

Eat Healthy

EGSG

Ans : ____________________

HIFS

Ans : ____________________

DALAS

Ans : ____________________

SREENG

Ans : ____________________

KLIM

Ans : ____________________

RUITFS

Ans : ____________________

Solve It

World Health Day is celebrated on April 7.
Help Monty match the following food items to the correct vitamins.

VITAMIN **B2**

VITAMIN **E**

VITAMIN **D**

VITAMIN **C**

Complete the Picture

Parts of this image have been left blank. Look at the picture, complete it, and then colour it.

Dot To Dot

Join the dots.

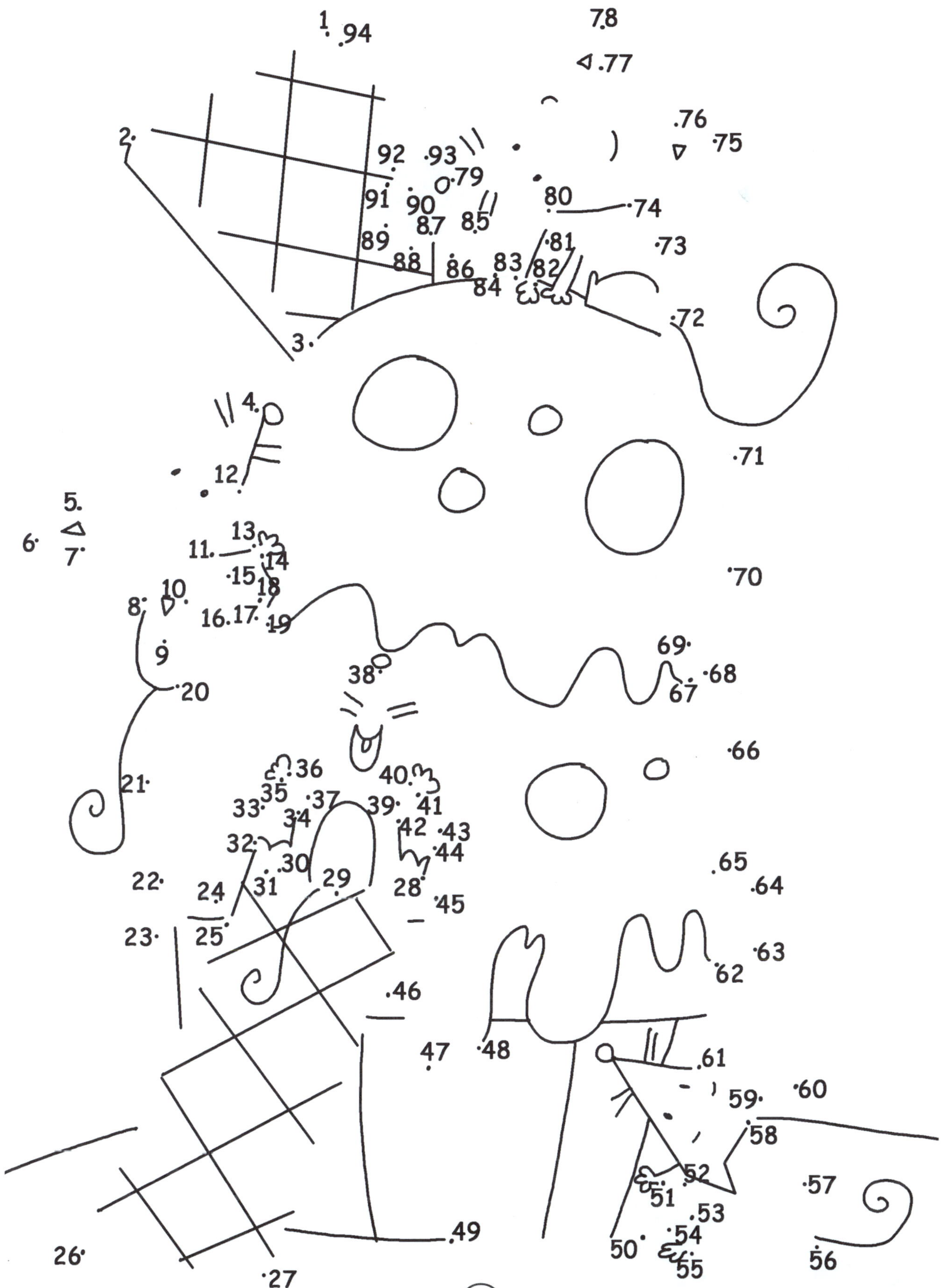

Maze

Help the fruits find their season.

Word Search

The name of a nut that helps boost your brain power is hidden in the grid below. Follow the instructions and find it.

Power Up!!!

A	B	K	X	G	K	K
G	L	X	B	G	X	G
G	B	M	X	K	X	X
K	G	G	O	P	P	B
X	K	G	P	N	G	B
X	X	X	P	B	D	P
B	X	B	K	P	X	B

Instructions:

First cross out all the Xs in the grid. Then cross out all the Gs and Ps. Now cross out the Bs and Ks. Unscramble the remaining alphabets to form the name of the nut.

Answer:

Did you know?

Sacramento and Chico, in California, are both known as the ______ capital of the world.

Complete the Picture

Parts of this image have been left blank. Look at the picture, complete it, and then colour it.

Colour using acrylic paints

Sequence

World Toilet Day is celebrated on November 19. Put the following steps used for hygienic sanitation, in the right sequence.

Complete the Word

Titli the butterfly has baked 10 cupcakes. Each contains an alphabet. Find them all and write them below.

Maze

World Post Day is celebrated on October 9. Ravi, the postman, has to collect a post from the postbox and deliver it to the house at the end of the maze. Help Ravi deliver the post.

Colour using bright colours

Solve It

It's National Mathematics Day on December 22. Calculate the change you would get if you buy the following items with the money shown near it.

Calculate Change

A '10

B

C

D

E

F

G

H

I

J

Colour using sketch pens

Complete the Picture

Parts of this image have been left blank. Look at the picture, complete it, and then colour it.

Use all the colours in your palette to colour me

Solve It

Kargil Victory Day is celebrated on July 26. Match the following badges to their respective titles.

- Havaldar
- Sipahi
- General
- Lieutenant
- Colonel
- Field Marshal

Hint: The higher the post, the more the decoration. A Sipahi is at the lowest rank, and the Field Marshal holds the most elevated position.

Dot To Dot

Join the dots according to the numbers and complete the picture.

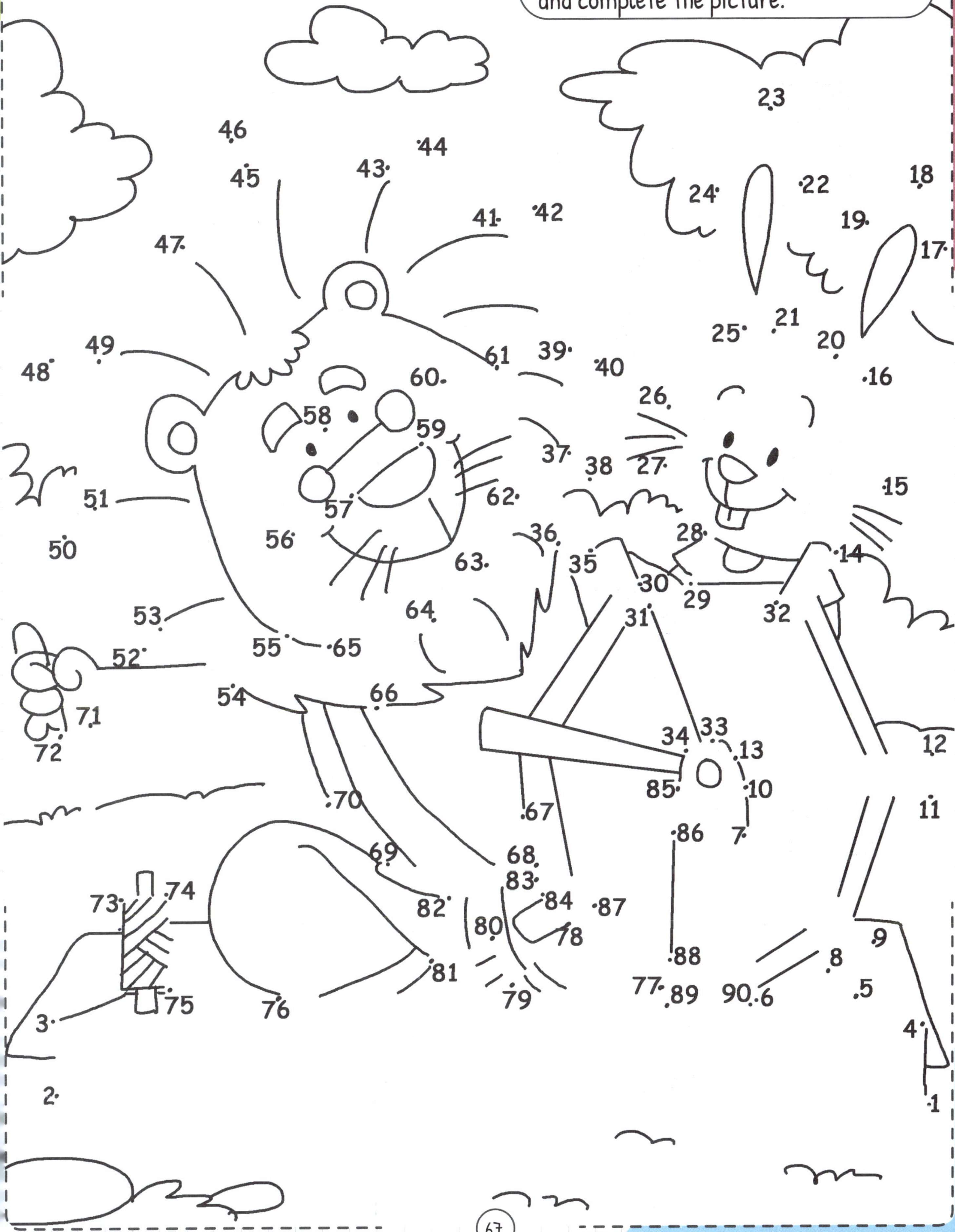

Solve It

International Labour Day is celebrated on May 1. Match the following occupations to their correct symbol.

Word Search

Mohit has set up an ice-lolly shop. He sells different flavours of ice-lollies that everyone can enjoy in Summer. The names of eight flavours are hidden in the grid below. Can you find them?

Flavour Hunt

C	H	E	R	R	Y	T	O	M	A
L	P	I	N	E	A	P	P	L	E
E	R	A	S	P	B	E	R	R	Y
M	I	M	B	L	A	C	K	B	O
O	R	A	N	G	E	G	A	Y	P
N	C	N	C	E	L	R	E	R	Y
K	A	G	B	U	T	A	S	C	S
S	R	O	H	G	R	P	I	O	T
S	T	R	A	W	B	E	R	R	Y

Maze

Help this science teacher find her way to the laboratory.

Map Quest

World Savings Day is celebrated on October 30. Saurav has saved money in his piggy bank. Guide him to the right counter.

1 - Behind the counter stands a man whom Saurav must approach.
2 - There's a small boy standing in front of the counter.
3 - Saurav doesn't have to go to the 'Loans' counter.
4 - There isn't a girl standing in front of the counter.

Maze

Help this police officer find her way to the thief.

Catch that thief

Odd One Out

Circle the tool that is not needed by the professionals.

Solve It

Find the correct Homophones

- Priya is tired after a long day at school. What does she need? ________

  A - break or B - brake

- Smoking in public places is not...

  ____

  A - Aloud or B - Allowed

- Ankur is lost. Should we turn...

  ____

  A - Right or B - Write

National Mathematics Day is celebrated on December 22. Choose the correct mathematical symbols for the equations below.

2 ☐ 10 = 20

14 ☐ 7 = 2

18 ☐ 5 = 13

26 ☐ 14 = 40

Math Symbols: + - X ÷

Map Quest

June 14 is World Blood Donor Day. Sahil has come to a blood donation camp with his mother. Use the hints given below to find out which of the following people will be eligible to donate blood.

The donor's haemoglobin level must be more than 12.5%
The donor should not suffer from diabetes, hypertension, cardiac arrest or kidney ailments.
The donor must be over 18 years of age and weigh more than 50 kg.

Maze

Help the skier find his way to the bottom of the slope.

SNOWY SLOPES

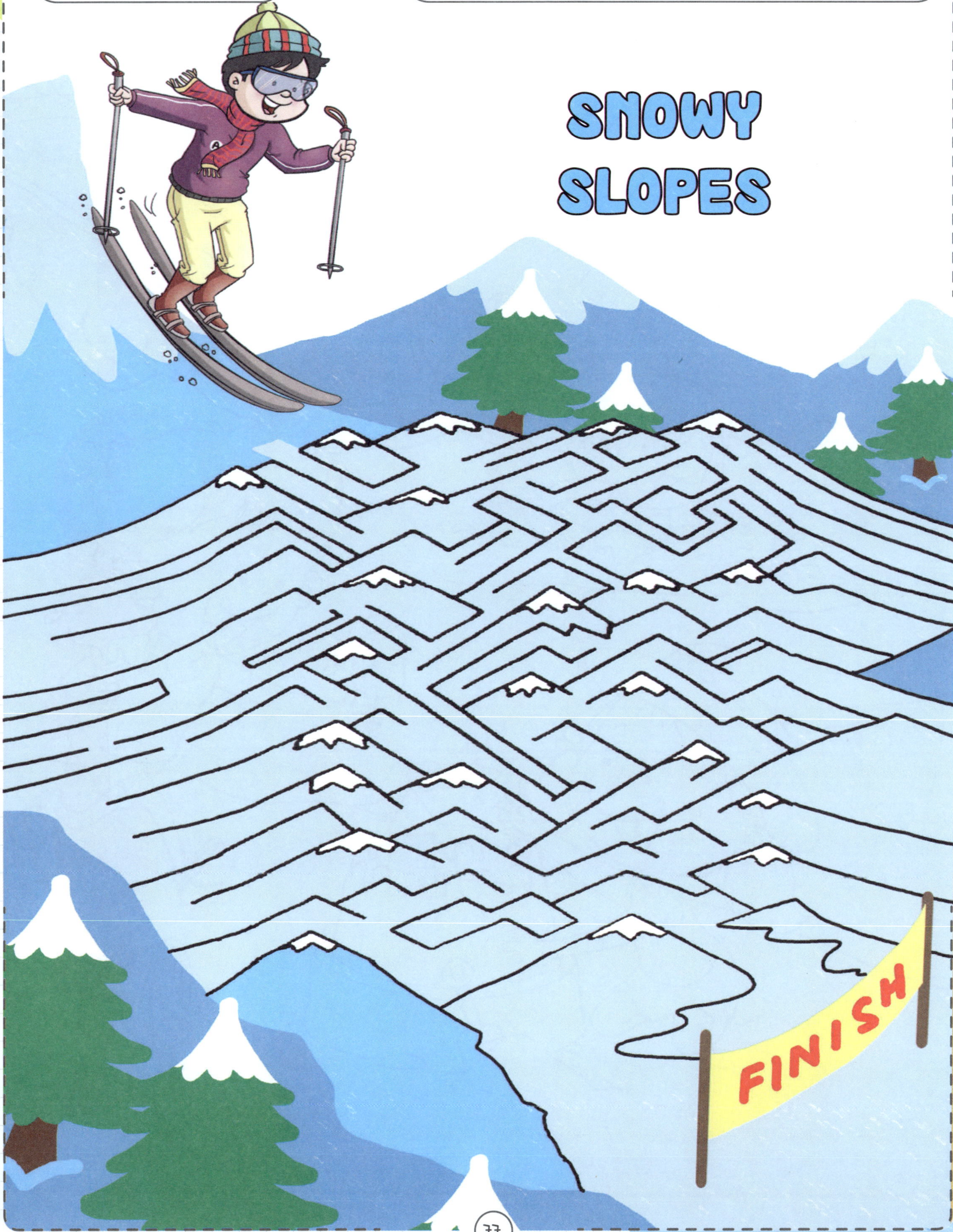

Colour using bright colours

If the s start to change their , it is probably autumn! Yes, that's when the s turn ,  and . They then fall off the s. The temperature drops and people wear s. Children pick up the fallen s for their scrapbooks. They also look for the seeds and s. They admire the s who have migrated from various places. The cool weather also makes fruits like s and s tastier. Autumn is an enjoyable season. So get your clothes made of . Start a  or  collection. And enjoy the tasty s.

Match

Dr. Duck and Gardener Goose have bumped into each other. Their tools have fallen off and got mixed up. Can you put the tools back in the correct bags?

Tools : stethoscope, spade, bag of seeds, cotton, watering can, thermometer, reflex hammer, doctor's torch, scythe, bandages, hoe, syringe, trowel

Dr. Duck's Bag: ______________________________

Gardner Goose's Bag: ______________________________

Play In May

May is a month full of fun. It begins with the letters “MA”, just like the names of other fun things. Fill in the blank spaces to know what they are. Then try and make them a part of your holidays.

Hint: Look at the illustrations if you need help.

MA○○C S○○WS

MA○K MAK○○G

MA○B○○S

MA○ R○○DI○G

MA○ARO○I NE○KL○CES

MA○ES

MA○R○ME

CHAMPAK MA○○Z○N○S

Word Search

Find the different languages spoken across the world, in the grid below.

M	R	A	Y	D	C	T	E	G	Q	S	G
C	K	N	S	U	I	A	U	T	I	O	N
P	A	S	H	T	O	U	W	M	N	C	R
A	Z	P	R	C	D	S	U	Q	D	T	U
O	A	A	E	H	E	B	R	E	W	A	S
S	K	Y	I	N	P	Y	N	R	A	C	Z
T	I	D	N	Z	E	A	E	G	P	L	B
H	N	C	O	U	N	T	R	Y	O	A	Q
U	I	B	E	I	D	K	Y	F	L	U	P
N	G	Y	P	R	F	R	I	S	I	A	N
S	B	A	R	S	N	A	M	Z	S	I	G
O	O	E	N	A	T	I	Q	N	H	L	V

1) P _ S H _ _

2) _ E _ RE _

3) KA _ _ K

4) F _ IS _ AN

5) I _ B _

6) PO _ _ SH

7) _ UT _ H

Colour using water colours

Word Link

Every word in this puzzle includes the word "RAIN" use the clues given alongside to complete all the words.

_ R A I N _ _ E _ D S

Rice, wheat, barley are grown here

_ R A I N _ _ O _ M

To think very hard

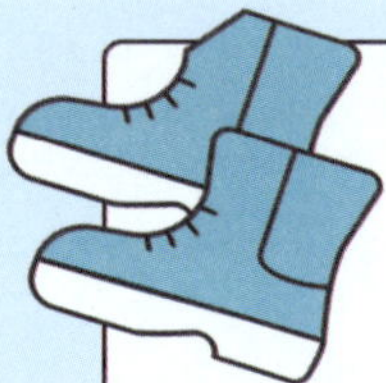

_ _ R A I N

To Tire one's self

_ R A I N _ I _ E

The Place where dirty water goes into

_ _ _ R A I N

A stretch of land

_ R A I N _ _

A person who is under training

M _ _ R A I N _

A very bad headache

Colour using cool colours

Complete the Picture

Parts of this image have been left blank. Look at the picture, complete it, and then colour it.

Colour using different shades of blue and yellow

Maze

Help the Olympic skier reach down the slope without colliding with any obstacles.

Dot to Dot

Find out the hidden joke that everyone's laughing about – connect the dots today!

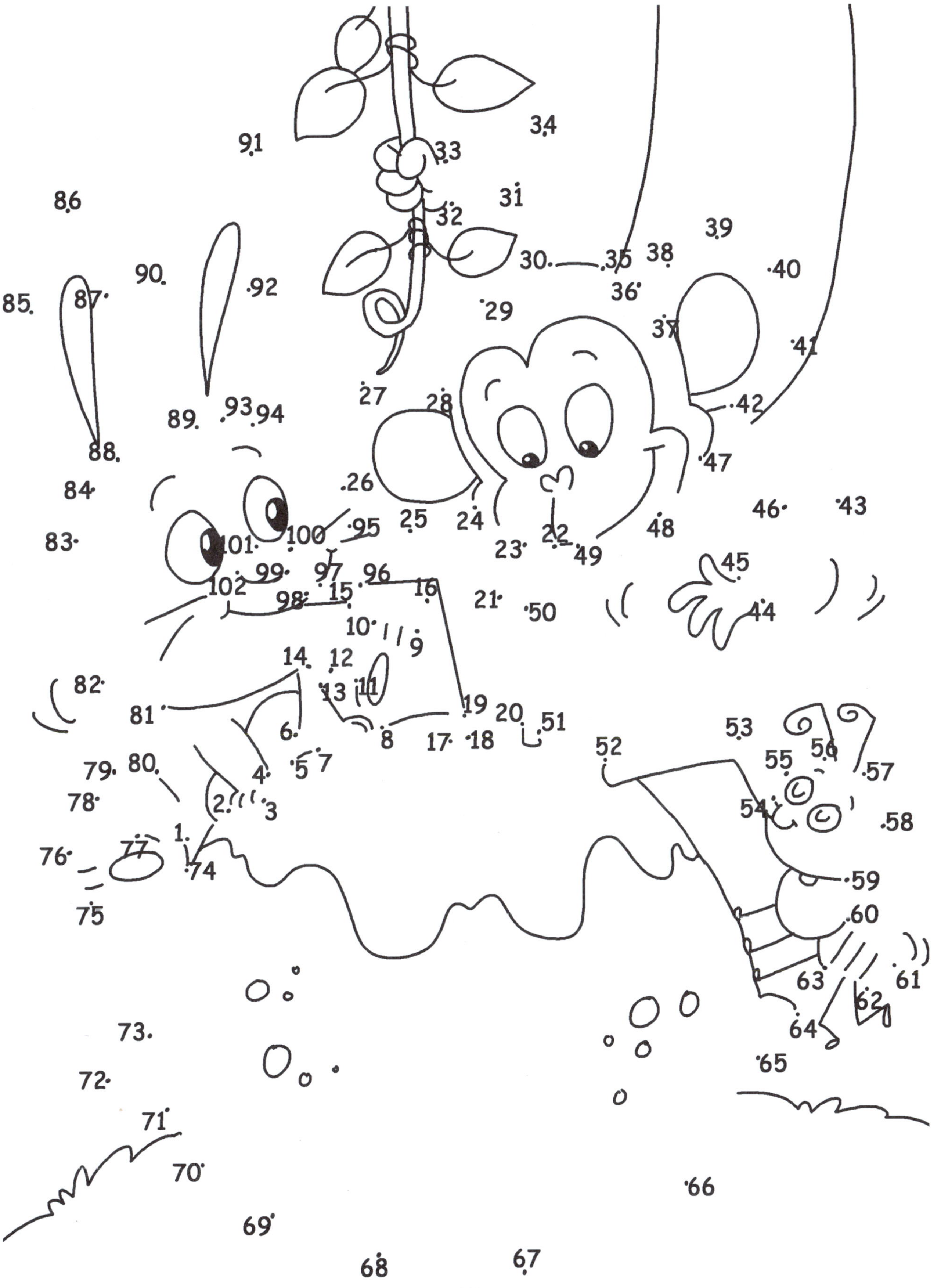

Nutty Snack

Cross out the letters following the instructions given below to find out the name of some nuts children love to roast and eat in winter.

P	H	S	V	T
D	Q	V	N	Q
J	E	J	U	P
V	D	Q	P	P
C	P	T	Q	D

Hint

First cross out all the Ps and Qs.
Then cross out all the Ds and Vs.
Then cross out all the Js.

Answer

Tune In

Write the first letter of the objects shown below to form the name given to the songs people sing during Christmas.

Answer:

Complete the Picture

Parts of this image have been left blank. Look at the picture, complete it, and then colour it.

Colour using poster colours

Dot to Dot

Join the dots to celebrate International Day of Happiness on March 20.

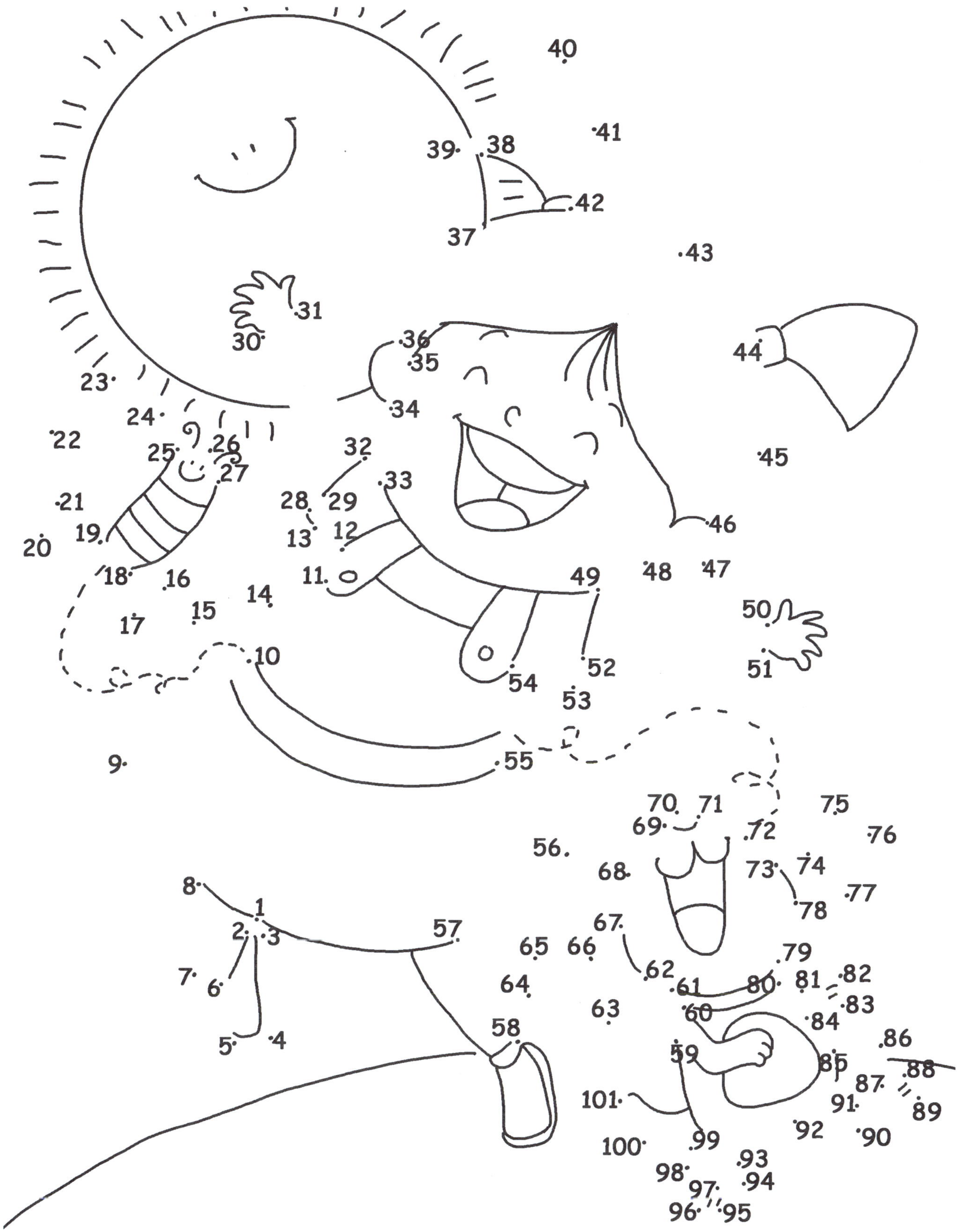

Colour using oil pastels

Decode Me

Can you find the name of this dark and gray cloud that is full of rain? Hint: Write the first alphabet of the objects shown below in the blanks. When you have all the alphabets, you will have the name!

Number Grid

This is a magical grid where numbers in each row and column add-up to 20. Fill in the numbers 2, 5, 6, and 7 in the empty boxes to complete the grid.

5	6		2	20
2	7	6		20
7		5	6	20
6	5	2	7	20
20	20	20	20	20

Name the Subjects

Subject names commonly originate from Greek language. The word 'logos' is a Greek word that means 'study of'. Guess the right subject names. We have solved the first one for you.

	Answer
1. The study of music	Musicology
2. The study of animals	
3. The study of Earth	
4. The study of ecosystem	
5. The study of ancient Egypt	

Colour using pastel tones

Reach the island

Help the rescue ship find its way to the island.

Dot to Dot

Join the dots to find out what everyone is laughing at.

Maze

Help these children from the future. Find their way to the time capsule.

Colour using paints of your choice

Maze

December 4 is celebrated as Navy Day. Rakesh is stuck on an island. Help the Indian Navy reach him.

Complete the Picture

August 9 is celebrated as International Day of the World's Indigenous People. Parts of this image have been left blank. Look at the picture, complete it, and then colour it.

Colour using yellow, green, red, brown and blue

Colour using neon colours

Word Search

The names of 8 activities you can enjoy in the mountains are hidden in the grid. Can you find them? Use illustrations if you need help.

Word Game

Every word in this puzzle includes the alphabets "TE". Use the clues given alongside to complete all the words.

WORD GAME

TE ___ ___ ___ ___ ___ ___ ___
(What you talk to your friends on.)

TE ___
(A hot drink)

___ ___ TE ___
(This liquid can make you wet and quench your thirst too.)

TE ___ 10
(The number after nine.)

___ ___ TE
(Not early.)

TE ___ ___
(A type of wood.)

TE ___ ___
(A group of players.)

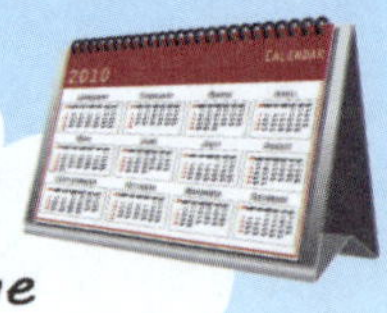

___ ___ TE
(A number on the calendar.)

TE ___ ___
(Like an exam.)

TE ___ ___
(A cloth house.)

*Answer on last page

Get into the holiday spirit with your favourite Christmas carol!

SING ALONG

This favourite Christmas carol has been written here using pictures and numbers instead of words. Can you read it?

Rudolph, the red-nosed 
had a very shiny .
And if you ever  him,
you would even say it .

All of the other 
used to  and call him names.
They never let poor Rudolph
join in any  games.

Then 1 foggy Christmas Eve
 came to say:
"Rudolph with your  so bright,
won't you guide my 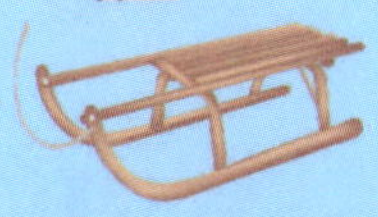 tonight?"

Then all the  loved him
as they shouted out with glee,
Rudolph the red-nosed ,
you'll go  in history!

Dot to Dot

Join the dots to find out what everyone is laughing at.

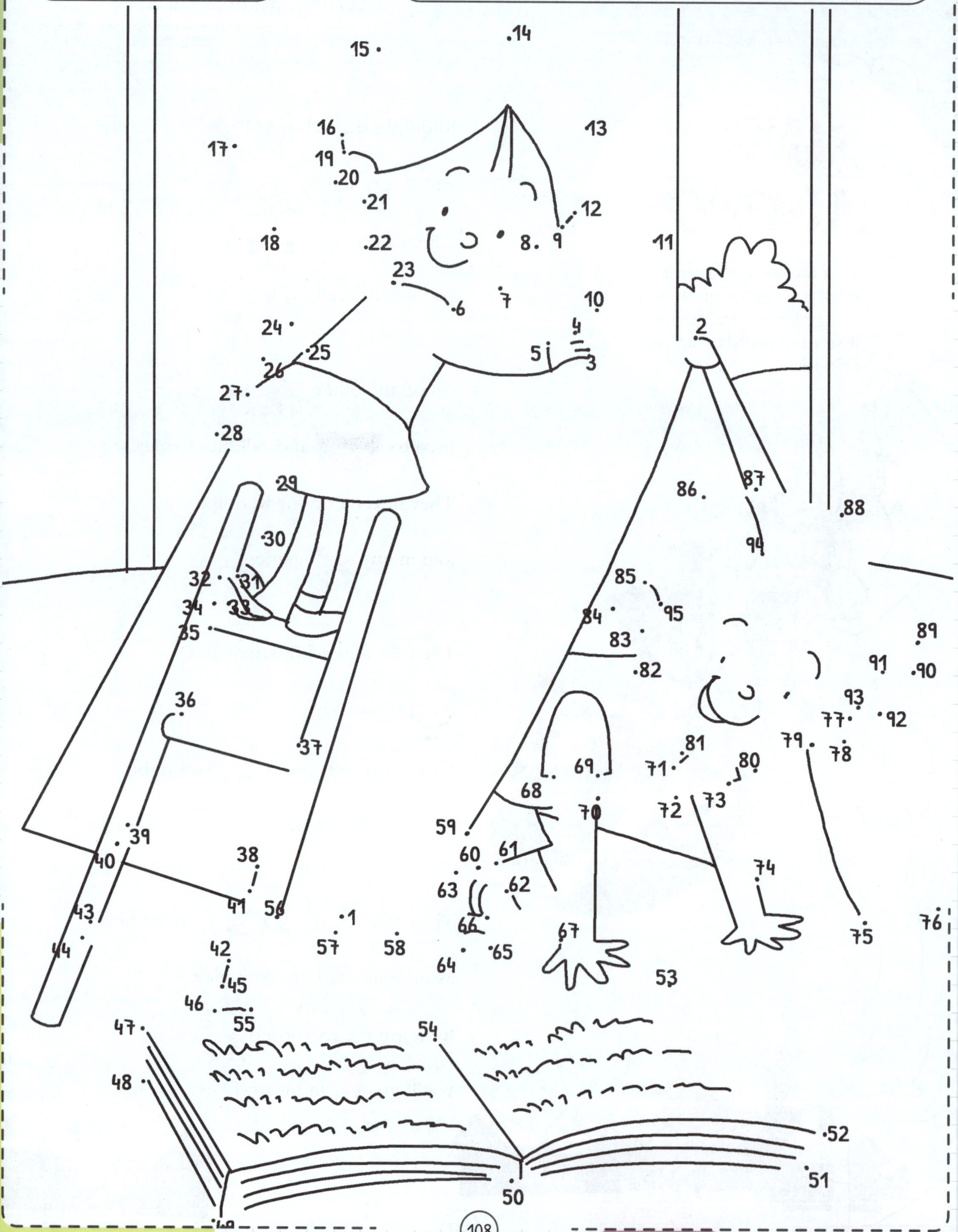

Colour using acrylic paints

National Sports Day is on August 29.

Dot to Dot

Let's play a fun game! Connect the dots and see what surprise is waiting for you at the end.

Maze

June 21 is World Music Day. Rahul is learning to play a classical musical instrument. Find out which instrument he plays by directing him out of the maze.

Colour using bright colours

Learn a Language

September 23 is the International Day of Sign Languages. With the help of the sign language bank, identify the words given below.

A B S F E D T

O L P J I M R

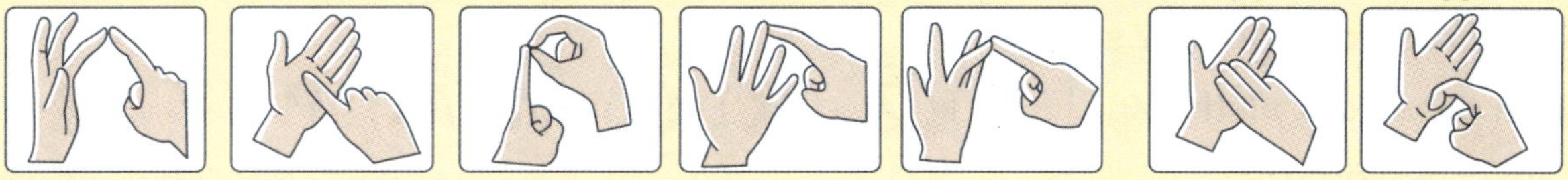

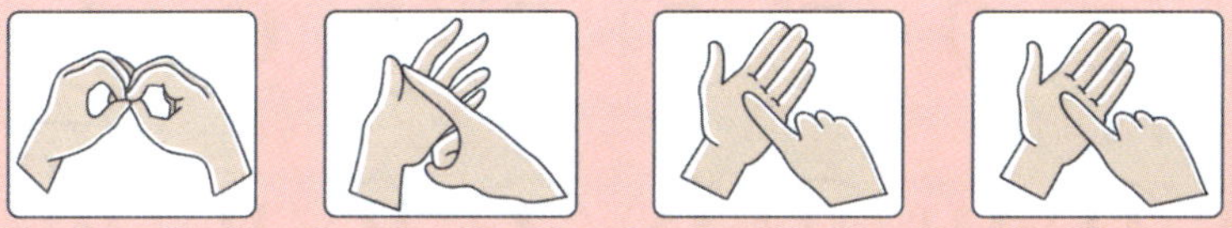

....

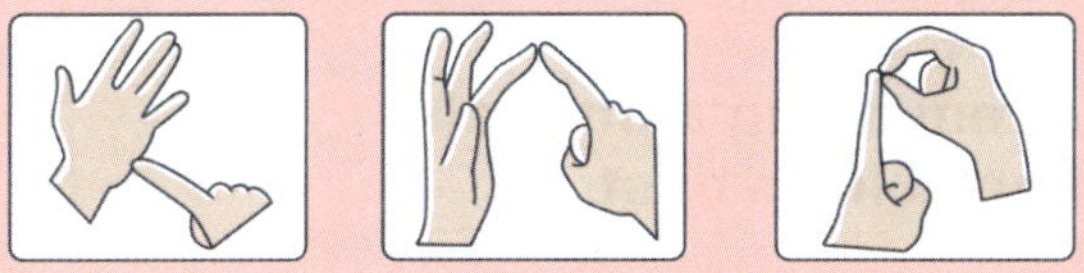

....

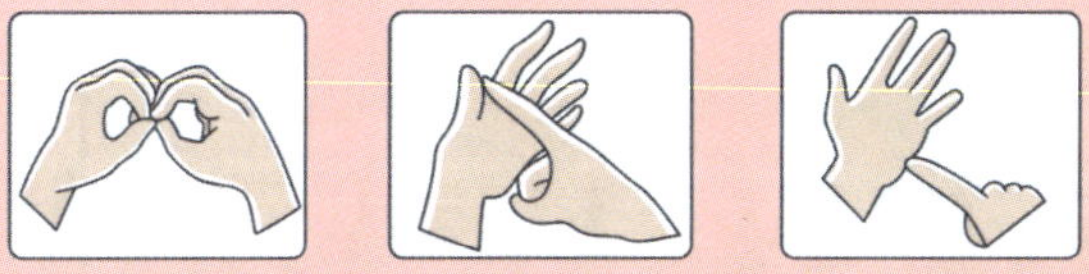

....

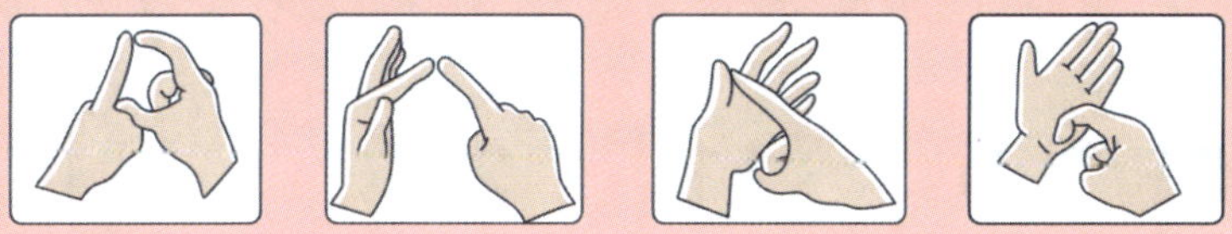

....

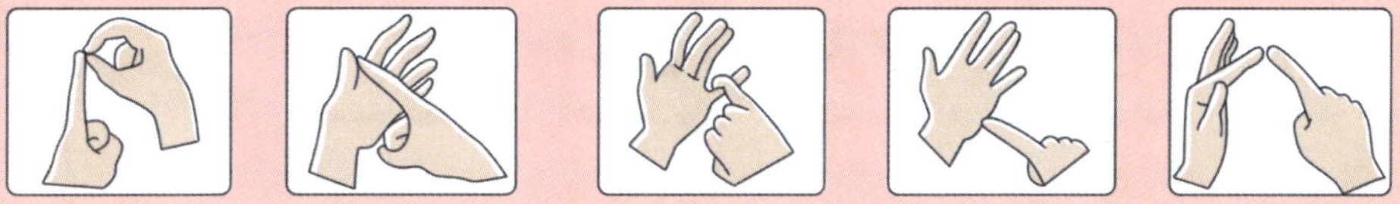

....

....

WORD SEARCH

What does Cheeku like best about Diwali? Follow the instructions to find the answer in the grid.

- First cross out all the Qs.
- Then cross out all the Ms.
- Then cross out all the Zs.
- Then cross out all the Xs.
- Now cross out Ps
- Then cross out all the Rs

Q	S	R	M	R	E	P	X	R	Q
P	Z	R	Q	M	M	P	T	Z	R
Z	Q	M	Z	R	Q	M	Z	Z	P
R	Z	Q	P	E	R	P	Q	S	Z
M	Q	W	R	Q	Z	R	R	P	Q

Unscramble the remaining alphabets to form what Cheeku likes best.
The answer is:

SUM IT UP!

Which 3 numbers should Jumpy add to get a total of 90?

40	6	11	22
62	73	85	27
0	0	69	79
50	13	30	19

Complete the Picture

Parts of this image have been left blank. Look at the picture, complete it, and then colour it.

Complete the Word

'J' For...

June starts with 'JU'! So do many other interesting words. Complete the following words that start with 'JU'.

Hint: Look at the pictures if you need help.

J U _ O

J U _ G _ _ _ G

J U _ _ B _ S

J U _ C _

J U _ G _

J U _ _ B _ X

J U _ P _ U I _

J U _ _ L _

*Answer on last page.

Dot to Dot

Join the dots according to the numbers and complete the picture.

Odd One Out

Exams are just around the corner. Help Kabir prepare for his exams by removing the odd items in each subjects.

Colour using sketch pens

Winter Connect

Find out which winter item belongs to whom.

Solve It

JUMPY'S STOLEN MONEY

Jumpy the monkey had withdrawn ₹7000 from the bank.
One day, after Jumpy had left home for work, Baddy the Fox and Laptu the Jackal entered his house and stole ₹2000. How much money does Jumpy have now?

Word Search

Christmas is celebrated on December 25. In the grid below, find the names of some of the ornaments used to decorate the Christmas tree.

1) S _ A _

2) _ NO _ MA _

3) C _ NDY C _ _ E

4) TI _ _ EL

5) RE _ ND _ ER _

6) S _ _ TA _ _ AUS

M	R	A	Y	B	C	T	E	G	T	S
C	I	D	U	H	A	M	K	U	N	A
H	P	Z	A	S	N	O	W	M	A	N
A	S	P	R	R	D	S	U	M	T	T
O	N	A	E	A	Y	G	I	A	N	A
S	A	Y	I	N	C	Y	N	R	A	C
T	I	D	N	E	A	W	E	G	I	L
H	N	Q	D	C	N	R	W	I	N	A
U	I	B	E	I	E	K	Y	S	I	U
N	T	Y	E	E	T	E	O	U	T	S
S	T	A	R	S	A	N	R	Z	A	I
O	L	E	S	I	T	I	N	S	E	L

Maze

This year, Diwali is being celebrated on November 7. Help Karan choose the right thread to light each cracker.

Colour using shades of pink, purple and red

Maze

Rohan is celebrating Friendship Day on August 5. Help him reach Ashok while making him meet all his friends along the way who he has to tie friendship bands.

Colour using your favourite paints

Dot to Dot

Complete the Picture

Parts of this image have been left blank. Look at the picture, complete it, and then colour it.

Colour using shades of orange, green, yellow and blue

Dot to Dot

Join the dots to find out what everyone is laughing at.

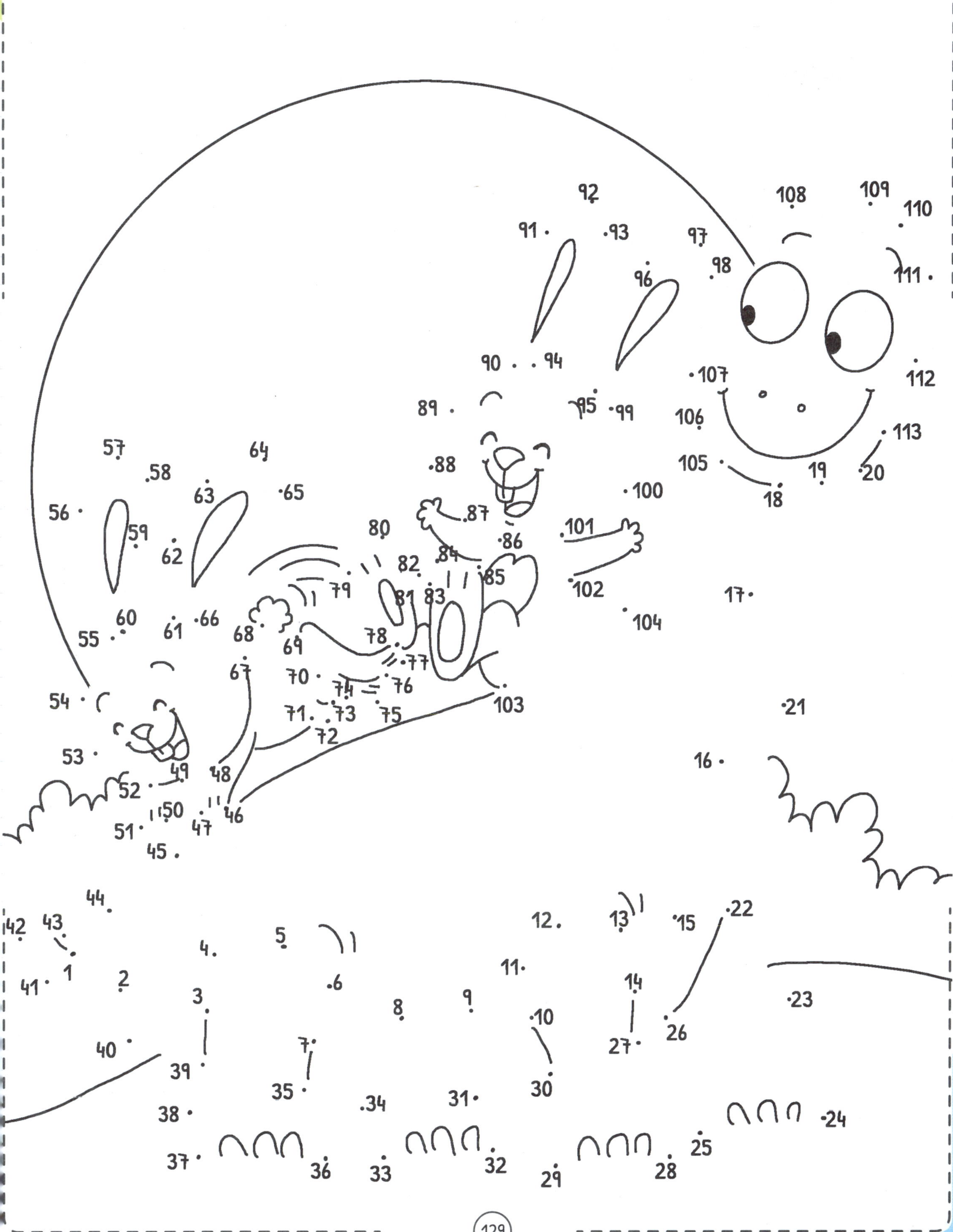

Complete the Picture

May 13 is Mother's Day. Parts of this image have been left blank. Look at the picture, complete it, and then colour it

Decode me

This giant computer has generated a special message using a secret code. Can you read it?

1=A, 2=B, 3=C, 4=D, 5=E, 6=F, 7=G,
8=H, 9=I, 10=J, 11=K, 12=L, 13=M, 14=N,
15=O, 16=P, 17=Q, 18=R, 19=S, 20=T, 21=U,
22=V, 23=W, 24=X, 25=Y, 26=Z

Answer:

_ _ _ _ _
_ _ _ _ _ _

Let's Search

Champakvan begins with "CH" and so do a lot of other interesting things. Complete the following words that start with "CH".

CH _ _ _ E

CH _ _ _ L _ _ E

CH _ _ C _ _ L

CH _ _ _ A _

CH _ _ P _ _ Z _ _

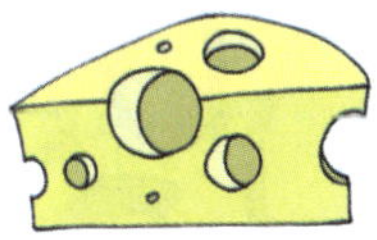

Maze

May 6 is World Laughter Day. A laughter carnival has come to Alfia's town. Help her visit all the events at the carnival before ending her day at the mime show.

Colour using crayons

Complete the Picture

Parts of this image have been left blank. Look at the picture, complete it, and then colour it.

Help this boy deposit the old bottles in the Recycling box.

Recycle it

Assist this young eco-warrior to keep our planet green!

*Answer on last page.

Game

Carbon dioxide and other gases emitted into the atmosphere cause Green House Effect, leading to global warming.

Stop Global Warming

You will need:

- ◊ Pegs for each player
- ◊ Dice

How to play:

- ◊ You can start when your dice rolls 2. Then roll it again and move your peg the number of spaces it shows.
- ◊ You will have to move back 2 spaces if you land on a polluting vehicle or factory.
- ◊ You can move ahead 2 spaces if you land on plants and trees.
- ◊ You will get an extra turn if you land on a recycling symbol.
- ◊ The player who reaches the last tile first, wins.

Note: The driveway for each plot is equivalent to one square space.

Zero to Hero

Things to do:

Get a haircut.
Get a new jacket.
Buy sun glasses.
Take dance classes.
Take acting classes.

Instructions:

To play this game, you have to count the spaces from one place to another and find out which is the shortest route. Mark the route Jumpy should take to do all the things in the shortest time.

Jumpy Monkey wants to audition for the role of a movie hero. Help him finish his tasks as soon as possible, and reach the Champakvan Studio.

*Answer on last page.

Answer

Page 3 :- Decode Me

She gets a chocolate float

Page 7 :-Complete the Word

1 - Beard, 2 - Bathtub,
3 - Vacation, 4 - Crowded,
5 - Butterfly, 6 - Starfish,
7 - Hotdog, 8 - Horseshoe

Page 10 :- Follow Me

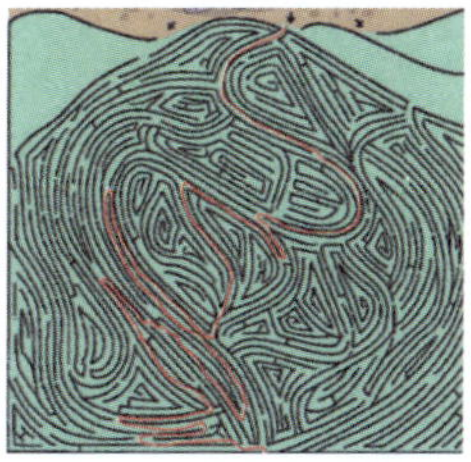

Page 13 :- Rebus

One day, a fox saw two meerkats. They were fighting over a fish. "Stop fighting," the fox said. "I will divide this fish for you." The meerkats believed the fox and let him pick up the fish. But to their surprise, the fox took the fish and ran away. "Oh no," the meerkats cried. "Had we not fought, or believed the fox, we would still have had our lunch!"

Page 15 :- Maze

Page 16 :- Maze

Page 17 :- Fill in the Blanks

1. A flight of bees
2. A murder of crows
3. A litter of cats
4. A clutch of chicks
5. A school of whales
6. A kettle of hawks
7. A pride of lions
8. A parliament of owls

Page 20 :- Maze

Page 22 :- Maze

Page 23 :- Solve It

Page 27 :- Decode Me

Decode Me - Butter Cup.

Page 30 :- Flower Search

Flower Search : Tulip, Rose, Daffodils, Daisy, Sunflower, Dandelion, Lily, Dahlia.

Busy Bee! : 41.

Page 31 :- Maze

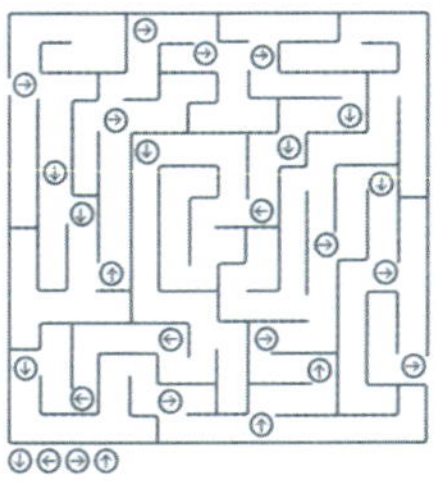

Page 32 :- Decode Me

Secret Code : Nightingale, Cardinal, Sparrow, Mockingbird and Finch.
Cross Out : Kiwi

Page 33 :- Solve It

Page 34 :-Word Search

B	E	S	W	B	U	A	S	D	E	B
O	L	H	E	A	T	P	R	P	L	K
D	E	O	S	R	T	A	B	C	E	H
H	P	F	A	T	E	H	P	U	R	A
G	H	I	L	A	K	C	A	O	B	J
A	A	L	K	H	A	M	P	I	A	U
Y	N	N	D	E	Y	K	I	I	N	R
A	T	T	A	J	M	A	H	A	L	A
N	A	V	A	X	H	A	A	N	A	H
M	B	R	P	U	S	U	Q	Y	L	O
Z	R	A	N	I	K	I	V	A	V	L

Page 34 :- Science Homework

Page 34 :- Fix the Recipe

A. Flour
B. Salt
C. Water
D. Oil

Page 36 :- Unscramble

1. Peacock
2. Emblem
3. Lotus
4. Gandhi
5. Banyan Tree
6. Mango
7. Hockey
8. Tiger

Page 37:- Maze

Page 40 :- Maze

Page 43 :- Word Search

Activity Therapy

Down: Cycling, Music, Reading, Swimming
Across: Yoga,Tennis, Karate
Run Along
2 and 4 appear four times. So the length of the race is 2x4=8 miles

Page 45 :- Solve It

WE WILL MISS YOU

Page 47 :- Maze

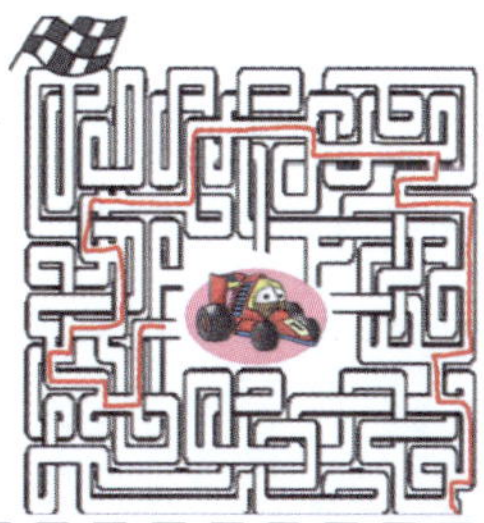

Answer

Page 49 :- Solve It

Change Challenge
Answers: 2, 5, 2, 5, 10, 10

In or Out Answers:
In: th, ch, w Out: ab, sc, tr,
Both: sh, p, sp

Page 50 :- Unscramble

Eat Healthy : FISH, GREENS, FRUITS, SALAD, MILK, EGGS.

Page 51 :- Solve It

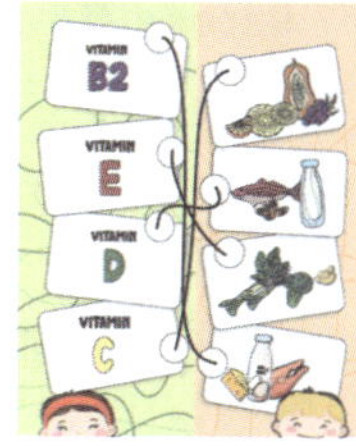

Page 54 :- Maze

Page 55 :- Word Search

Power up – ALMOND

Page 58 :- Sequence

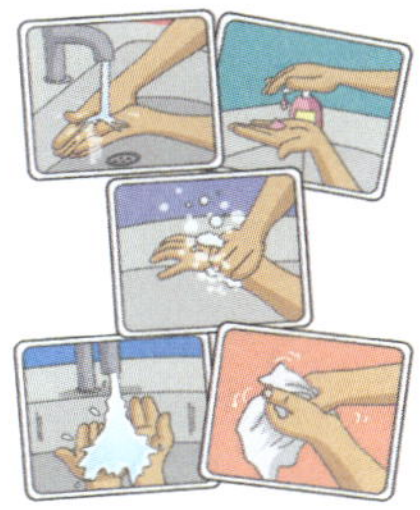

Page 59 :-Complete the Word

Sweet Words : FRIENDSHIP

Page 60 :- Maze

Page 62 :- Solve It

A.`10  B.`150
C.`4  D.`8
E.`15  F.`0
G.`5  H.`2
I.`10  J.`20

Page 68 :- Solve It

1. E 2. F 3. D
4. A 5. C 6. B

Page 71 :- Maze

Page 72 :- Map Quest

Page 73 :- Maze

Page 74 :- Odd One Out

Page 75 :- Solve it

1 – break, 2 – allowed, 3 – right

2 X 10 = 20
14 ÷ 7 = 2
18 - 5 = 13
26 + 14 = 40

Page 76 :- Map Quest

Page 77 :- Maze

Page 79 :-Rebus

Autumn is here! : It the leaves start to change their colours, it is probably autumn! Yes, that's when the leaves turn red, yellow and brown. They then fall off the trees. The temperature drops and people wear sweaters. Children pick up the fallen leaves for their scrapbooks. They also look for the seeds and pinecones. They admire the birds who have migrated from various places. The cool weather also makes fruits like apples and oranges tastier. Autumn is an enjoyable season. So get your clothes made of wool. Start a leaf or nut collection. And enjoy the tasty pumpkins

Page 80 :- Match

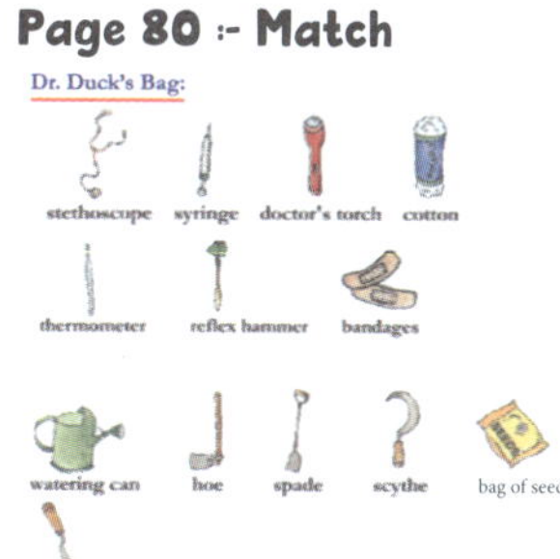

Page 81 :- Complete the Word

Play in May
Magic shows, mask making, marbles, map reading, macaroni, necklaces, mazes, macramé and magazines.

Page 82 :- Word Search

M	R	A	Y	D	C	T	E	G	Q	S	G
C	K	N	S	U	I	A	U	T	I	O	N
P	A	S	H	T	O	U	W	M	N	C	R
A	Z	P	R	C	D	S	U	Q	D	T	U
O	A	A	E	H	E	B	R	E	W	A	S
S	K	Y	I	N	P	Y	N	R	A	C	Z
T	I	D	N	Z	E	A	E	G	P	L	B
H	N	C	O	U	N	T	R	Y	O	A	Q
U	I	B	E	I	D	K	Y	F	L	U	P
N	G	Y	P	R	F	R	I	S	I	A	N
S	B	A	R	S	N	A	M	Z	S	I	G
O	O	E	N	A	T	I	Q	N	H	L	V

Page 84 :- Complete the Word

GRAINFIELDS, BRAINSTORM, TRAINEE, DRAINPIPE , STRAIN, MIGRAINE, TERRIAN

Page 88 :- Maze

Answer

Page 90 :- Complete the Word

Nutty snack : Chestnut
Tune In : Carols

Page 95 :- Decode Me

Decode Me
Nimbus

Name the Subjects
Zoology, Geology, Ecology and Egyptology

5	6	7	2	20
2	7	6	5	20
7	2	5	6	20
6	5	2	7	20
20	20	20	20	20

Page 97 :- Maze

Page 99 :- Maze

Page 101 :- Maze

Page 105 :- Word Search

Adventure Hunt : HIKING, CAVING, ROCKCLIMBING, SKIING, TREKKING,
CAMPING, SNOWBOARDING, RAPPELLING.

Page 107 :- Rebus

Rudolph, the red-nosed reindeer had a very shiny nose. And if you ever saw him, you would even say it glows. All of the other reindeer used to laugh and call him names. They never let poor Rudolph join in any reindeer games. Then one foggy Christmas Eve Santa came to say: "Rudolph with your nose so bright, won't you guide my sleigh tonight?" Then all the reindeer loved him as they shouted out with glee, Rudolph the red-nosed reindeer, you'll go down in history!

Page 111 :- Maze

Page 113 :- Learn a language

1. Ball | 2. Top | 3. Bat | 4. Dear |
5. Paste | 6. Pests

Page 114 :- Word Game

Sweets

Page 116 :- Complete the Word

Judo, Juggling, Jujubes, Juice, Judge, Jukebox, Jumpsuit and Jungle

Page 118 :- Math

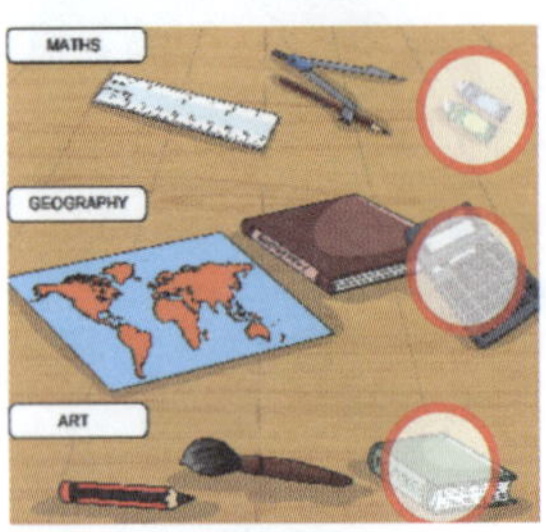

Page 121 :- Solve It

Jumpy's
Stolen Money 5000

M	R	A	Y	B	C	T	E	G	T	S
C	I	D	U	H	A	M	K	U	N	A
H	P	Z	A	S	N	O	W	M	A	N
A	S	P	R	R	D	S	U	M	T	T
O	N	A	E	A	Y	G	I	A	N	A
S	A	Y	I	N	C	Y	N	R	A	C
T	I	D	N	E	A	W	E	G	I	L
H	N	Q	D	C	N	R	W	I	N	A
U	I	B	E	I	E	K	Y	S	I	U
N	T	Y	E	E	T	E	O	U	T	S
S	T	A	R	S	A	N	R	Z	A	I

Page 122 :- Maze

Page 124 :- Maze

Page 131 :- Decode Me

Decode Me : Happy Diwali.

Let's Search : Cheese, Chocolate, Charcoal, Cheetah, Chimpanzee.

Page 132 :- Maze

Page 135 :- Maze

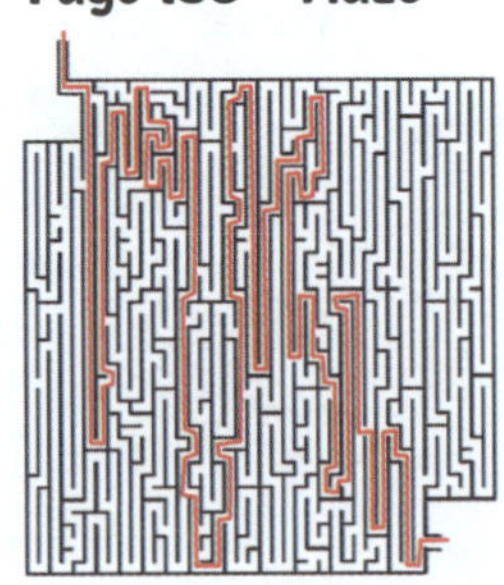